Trancers

Margarita Felices

MARGARITA FELICES

TRANCERS

For Mum and Puri – as always.

Excerpt from Trancers

One of the patients had left his room and was walking over to him. Travis let out a feeble scream as the man, who was in a near catatonic state got closer. His grey complexion shimmered in the lights of the corridor, his eyes were sunken and grey and his bald head was bent over to the side as he stared at Travis. His feet shuffled on the tiles of the hospital floor as he walked towards him. He seemed determined to get close to him. His arms were outstretched and his thin long fingers moved quickly in an attempt to snare him. If Travis could pick any horror genre that he hated above all else it would be zombies, and this patient was just too close to the real thing.

Travis took a quick side step and held out his arms to stop the patient getting too close. He jumped aside and got around him with the agilities of a trained gymnast and headed back to his own room, closed the door and propped up a chair under the handle to make sure no one could get in.

TRANCERS

Copyright

Trancers

Books to Go Now Publication

Copyright © Margarita Felices 2017

Books to Go Now

http://www.bookstogonow.com

Cover Design by Romance Novel Covers Now

http://www.romancenovelcoversnow.com/

For information on the cover illustration and design, contact bookstogonow@gmail.com

First Paperback Edition June 2018

ISBN-13: 978-1720599418

ISBN-10: 1720599416

Warning: the unauthorized reproduction or distribution of this copyrighted work is illegal. Criminal copyright infringement, including infringement without monetary gain, is investigated by the FBI and is punishable by up to 5 years in prison and a fine of $250,000. All rights reserved. No part of this book may be reproduced or transmitted in any form without written permission from the publisher, except by a

MARGARITA FELICES

reviewer who may quote brief passages for review purposes.

This book is a work of fiction and any resemblance to any person, living or dead, any place, events or occurrences, is purely coincidental. The characters and story lines are created from the author's imagination and are used fictitiously.

If you are interested in purchasing more works of this nature, please stop by
www.bookstogonow.com

TRANCERS

OTHER STORIES BY MARGARITA FELICES

JUDGEMENT OF SOULS 1: Origin
JUDGEMENT OF SOULS 2: Call of The Righteous
JUDGEMENT OF SOULS 3: Kiss at Dawn
The Psychic
Story of My Heart
A Christmas Embrace
Ordinary Wins

MARGARITA FELICES

TRANCERS

CHAPTER ONE

The sun that had blazed above the desert landscape all day had maybe another hour before it would start its descent from the sky as Travis Williams drove down Interstate 10. The skies had already begun to turn into a spectacular display of yellows and oranges and reds. The kind of colours you'd expect to see as you approached the outer rims of the desert. The highways were deserted. Even the mix of ominous birds that kept up with him and flew over his car as he drove for miles, had gone to leave him with only his thoughts and emotions.

Travis could have easily been mistaken for an actor or a fashion model or even a rock star. He certainly had that sought after chiselled chin, high cheek bone, pouty lipped appearance that attracted attention. He was almost five foot eight with a slim, but muscled physique that turned the eye of many of the girls he passed in pubs or clubs when he was out with friends each week—and even some of the men. His hair was slightly longer than he'd normally have it. He'd decided some weeks before, to grow it out a little. For his trip to America, he wanted the whole Hollywood bad boy look. He'd even got a tan from one of those fake tan shops that he'd always hated but thought he'd use just this once. He didn't even notice that after a week of using a liquid self-tanner that he no longer needed the top up, until he scrubbed himself in the shower one morning and realised it wasn't washing off. His facial hair was just the right length, it skimmed his chin and face and his dark brown eyes suited the entire look. He wore black jeans, black trainers and a white tee-shirt in an almost cliché American look that he hoped would not make him stand out too much as a tourist. And of course, the dark-rimmed aviator sunglasses completed his look.

He'd been in America for eleven days and had so far managed to rush from one place to the next, to make sure he got to visit some capital cities and famous landmarks he'd wanted to see before the holiday was over. He flew from London to New York, then a local flight to Chicago, another to Washington and from there back to New York. But now it was time for his real dream and the reason why he'd turned down so many night outs and mini getaways with his friends back home, in order to save his money. He was about to drive across an American desert to end up in Los Angeles - with only a few planned stops at some of the local hotels and motels along the way—and then, only if he had to.

Travis bought a cheap flight from New York to Washington and from there he took a local flight to Baton Rouge. When he arrived, he organised a hire car that would take him away from the busy streets in exchange for the blistering heat of the desert and the long, long highways.

His starting point was the capital of the state of Louisiana. Baton Rouge ran alongside the banks of the Mississippi River, on the south-eastern side of Louisiana. It still had a very strong French influence that dated back from its occupation in the seventeenth century. The design and build of some of its oldest residences wouldn't be out of place if they were currently located in the middle of Paris. The earliest, and most historic landmark, was a fort. Built in the city in 1719, the locals funded any maintenance it needed and it paid its way by attracting tourists, not just from the neighbouring states, but from foreign countries too, and especially when it held its annual parade. They would decorate the fort in flags and coloured bunting and in the evenings, hold spectacular fireworks displays that lit up the skies.

That year, the city was gearing up for its two hundredth anniversary. Baton Rouge had started its preparations with bunting and lights and mile upon mile of colourful flowers in huge painted pots, that lined the streets and roads and smaller ones for the balconies of apartment complexes as well as the hotels, bars and other entertainment establishments. It looked like a New Orleans Mardi Gras.

Travis decided that his journey would start with a drive alongside the river he'd heard so much about. And it was one of the things he could tick off his to-do list. Actually, his bucket list was to ride on one of the steamer ships but as it happened, the three days that he spent there, they were out of action while they got them serviced, painted and decorated for the festivities. But by also taking that route along the banks, it meant that he could avoid the huge refinery that gave Baton Rouge a strange aroma. It often intensified when certain strong winds blew—which was mostly around hurricane season. For the locals, it acted as a sort of bizarre hurricane warning, hours before the actual thing hit the ground.

Travis stayed in Baton Rouge for just three days and left promptly after breakfast in the hopes that he could make a far enough distance before it got too dark. It would take him at least four days to drive across the country. He hadn't driven that long in the US yet, and he had definitely not done so it at night, which seemed like a possibility if he could manage it. To ease the stress of the travel, he made himself a detailed schedule that would cover as much of the country as possible. If he was going to make it to Los Angeles by the following weekend, he would know how long to drive for and how limited his rest stops had to be.

Six months earlier, he planned the whole journey, down to the very last minute. It would take at least thirty hours of constant driving and if he was lucky, he could do eight to ten hours a day, with just the usual, only-stop-if-anything-looks-too-interesting-to- -pass-by every now and again. Also, for food, petrol and a suitable toilet break so he didn't have to pee in the desert, and then be quickly back on the road again.

His journey was to take him from Baton Rouge to Lafayette to Beaumont to Pasadena, near Houston, and avoid the heavily populated traffic areas, onto Interstate 90 and straight to Phoenix. Next it would be through to El Paso - straight on to connect with Interstate 10 and then - to Los Angeles. And then maybe, if he made good time, to San Diego.

His only pre-booked sleep stops were in Pasadena and Phoenix, but he made a note of some others that he would pass on the road, should he need to stop for the night before his scheduled stops. But those were mainly so that he didn't have to end up sleeping in the car, in the middle of nowhere. Of course, if he was home in Wales, he wouldn't have been as nervous of the drive. He often worked late and he enjoyed the solitude of the roads at night. And the plan seemed so perfect as he organised them all in his head and then on paper. But now he was here, the US was different. In some parts, it was always busy with large trucks – some eighteen wheelers and a few bigger, passed him on several occasions going so fast that they made his car and the road shake like mini earthquakes. And all of them demanded to take over the roads whether you wanted to give way and move over to them or not. At least twice, he'd had to swerve onto the side of the road in order to stay on the highway.

And some of the roads were dark, really dark, and it didn't help when Travis's eyes started to droop after the first night. Maybe it was the hot air of the day and the humid temperatures of the evening, or the tedious drive along a highway that seemed never-ending. But fortunately for him, up ahead in the distance. He could see the lights of a motel and decided to stop for the night, an unscheduled stop for a trip that might not hold fast to his expected and detailed plans.

After breakfast the next morning, Travis felt refreshed and excited to take on another full day of driving. He'd driven for seven hours the day before, instead of his scheduled ten for the first night, so he had to catch up or he'd never make LA on the day that he wanted.

The breeze that entered the car via the open windows was hot and humid, even for that time of the morning. But Travis had a choice. He could drive with the windows open, his arm out and relaxed enjoying the strange smells of food, flowers, diesel, tarmac and the change in air quality, or he could close the windows, turn on the air conditioning and miss everything about America that he wanted to experience. He wanted to feel and smell every sensation. He'd read in his research, that you could tell what state you were in, simply by the smell of the plants and flowers or the pop-up food vendors. And he wasn't going to miss that.

He'd never seen such plants growing on the sides of a road before. Saguaro cactus that he'd seen in hundreds of western films, stood up proud, sometimes ominous in their shapes and sizes—especially at night. Different coloured cholla with bright flowers and their deadly sharp thorns, blanketed some areas and then disappeared entirely, only to come back farther down the road in different vibrant colours, each one more flamboyant than the last. The smells as he drove past were sweet, inviting and tempting, like the smell of vanilla when you really craved for something sweet. Mum would love these plants in her garden, thought Travis. Perhaps when he got home, he'd look some up and make her that rock garden she was always asking for. The colours were certainly something that she would love, so bright, so flamboyant and yet so unusual.

He turned the dial on the radio to keep alert and laughed as it went from classic rock to country to gospel and even to Hispanic music within a few minutes. Even an evangelical preacher spouted the Good Word like the scene of an old Deep South film, telling listeners they were all going to hell. Travis fiddled with the dials and tried to find something that he could enjoy while driving, and managed to get the end of an Eagles track. Perfect on-the-road music. He settled back in the drivers' seat and smiled. It was everything he had imagined. It was just him in a car, the open roads and a radio station that played some of his favourite songs. He might never go back home.

He spent most of that day driving alongside timeless desert scenery, and it was as spectacular as he'd always dreamt it would be. But on day two, after an already long seven hours, it became just another cactus, just another shrub and just another mound of rock formations. When the sun went down, all he could see was the creepy shapes of the cacti and he tried not to stare at them for too long. The map he was using and his schedule were open on the front seat next to him, so he knew that just over that next ridge, was another motel. He'd marked it on his map as a possible stop if he felt that the journey had started to become too tiring. Then he heard the BOOM of a thunderclap a mile away in front of him, so loud that it shook the very ground he drove on. He swerved slightly onto the edge of the road, in shock at the echoing rumble that seemed to be on top of him, without any warning. But it was the light show in the distance that finally made him pull over.

The lay-by was perfectly timed. He got out of the car and sat on the bonnet as he looked on in awe at the spectacular light show that illuminated the dark skies around him. Cloud to ground white lightning hit the desert sands to send exploding lights of dust particles into the air like the embers of a fire. Then two anvil crawlers going in opposite directions, created the next spectacular array. Travis's eyes widened as he muttered, "Wow!" in astonishment. He was sure that one was at least a close strike and must have done some damage to whatever it had hit. Or maybe it just left a fiery crater somewhere out in the desert? With two more thunderous roars from the heavens, it was all over. Storms back home would never look the same to him again. At least no rain came with this storm, although it had helped tone down the humidity of the evening,

Back on the road, he decided to speed down the road to make up for the time he'd just spent parked. In the darkness, he hadn't realised that the roads rose up and then dipped deep down and then rose up again for the next few miles.

As Travis rose to the top of the road and then began his climb down, he saw bright headlights of an eighteen wheeler in front of him. The truck driver swerved and so did he. The car flipped into the air and came down with all four tyres back on the sand and into a huge cloud of sand and dirt.

It was a good twenty minutes before Travis

blinked and let go of the steering wheel. He looked back out into the dark night and road. The highway was quiet again, and nothing passed by him as he recalled the near miss and finally exhaled. Even the truck was gone. It seemed the driver didn't care enough to stop and see if he was all right or not. Had the trucker even seen him? The cab was so big and so high, maybe he hadn't. He had no idea how he'd missed the truck. He had no idea how he'd steered the car across the highway into the sand and how it had landed right side up. All he knew was that he was alive, shaken and in need of a good strong drink and a lie down. So he started up the car and drove back onto the highway, slower than before and very aware of what else may lie ahead of him if he didn't pay attention again.

It wasn't too far in the distance that he saw the luminance of a neon light. It flickered at first until he got closer and then saw it was a sign that pointed down a dark road. The sign blinked on and off with a giant white HO, but the rest of it was not lit. A hotel perhaps? He thought as he tried to focus on it? Or even a hostel? He didn't much care as long as it had a bed and a mini bar.

He turned down the dirt road and headed toward the lights of a building that was about two miles away.

He drove through two giant iron gates, down the driveway and as soon as he reached the front of the building, he got out of the car. Almost immediately, a woman came out of the double doors and greeted him.

She stood in the doorway with a peculiar glow from the reception lights behind her. Almost five foot five tall, her dark hair was tied back in a matron-like bun. She slouched with her arms folded, as he walked over to her. Her slender figure was obviously overshadowed by a top-heavy bust that seemed out of place for the rest of her body. She wore a medical uniform in royal blue with a white collar and short sleeves which skimmed to just below her knee and topped off the whole look with regulation flat black shoes and tights. But it was her eyes that Travis noticed first as he came close. They were a bright blue sapphire colour that sparkled out into the darkness. They made him feel somewhat…comforted, as if he was walking into his mother's arms. Her smile seemed genuine and equally as inviting.

"You look shaken, are you okay? Come inside,"

she said with a smile. "We had a room just become vacant this morning. It has an en suite and—"

Travis interrupted. "To be honest, I'd sleep on a blanket on the floor right now."

"Have you been driving long?"

"Most of the day…I just…I'm feeling so tired right now, I just need to sleep."

"Well sure come this way. I'll get you all signed in and take you to your room."

Travis followed her in but something made his stop and turn around. It sounded like voices, a distant echo of a sound that he couldn't make out, but was still familiar.

"Are you coming?" asked the woman.

"Yes, I'm sorry." He was puzzled and confused as he followed her. "For a minute, I thought I heard someone call my name."

CHAPTER TWO

When Travis woke up the next day, the sun blazed through the slats of the white blinds in his room. He looked at the clock on the wall and hoped it was wrong. A glance at his watch confirmed that it was already 11:30 p.m. He groaned. He was already behind his own schedule. The near miss from the previous night, slammed back into his head like a bad dream. He'd been so sure that truck was going to hit him. Perhaps there was someone up there smiling down on him at the time, divine intervention. Whatever it was, he was grateful and humbled and very, very relieved. Maybe driving for so long each day wasn't such a good idea after all. But at least now that he'd gotten enough sleep, he'd be able to drive until nightfall and then he could find another hotel and bed down. Schedule or not, what good was the whole adventure if he wasn't going to be around to enjoy it?

He got dressed quickly, grabbed his rucksack and left the room. Not far from his room, he noticed signs that gave directions to different areas. One read "Coffee Area." He could at least stop and have breakfast before setting off and perhaps thank the nurse for making him so welcome.

The morning coffee served in the breakfast room wasn't as nice as the one he'd gotten from the diners he'd stopped in, but it would have to do. And the breakfast wasn't bad. It was unusual to find a place in the US that served a full traditional English breakfast, something he'd been craving for a while. In fact, it was the first thing he'd thought of as he left his room and followed the coffee signs. After he'd stacked his plate and devoured the lot, he helped himself to another roll, stuffed it with bacon and wrapped it up in a tissue for later. He placed it in his rucksack and headed outside to his car. That's when he saw it. The whole right side of the car and the roof had been smashed in and The one tire was almost flat. But how had he managed to drive so far with the car in this state? He didn't even remember getting hit by anything to give the car those sorts of dents.

The same woman who greeted him when he arrived the previous evening, walked out of the building and stood next to him. "I noticed that last night too. I was just telling the porters that I didn't know how you managed to drive here with it in that state."

"I was thinking that same exact thing," Travis said, still shocked.

She turned and extended her hand and Travis gave it a friendly shake. "I'm Nurse Watkins, by the way. I'm the Head Nurse and also the Administrator of this facility."

"Travis Williams." He turned back to the car. "That's so odd," he said, confused. "I remember that a truck was in my lane and it nearly hit me. Then, all I remember is waking up on the side of the road and he hadn't hit me, but I wasn't half shaking. I must have swerved and spun and I think I may have hit a rock, but I was fine. The car made it as far as here without a problem. That doesn't look like it'd get me a mile to anywhere."

"Well, you're going to have a big problem if you leave here with that flat." She continued, "And you'll have to get the car repaired or the cops will pull you over. They don't take too kindly to wrecked cars being driven on their highway. Why don't I get one of the porters to sort it out for you? There's a garage up the road. I'll get one of them to give them a call and get a mechanic over here to see about it, while you enjoy some food. You can join the other patients in the dining room if you'd like some dinner. If you go through the double doors and then to the left, you can help yourself to the buffet or you can ask the chef for anything you want. They can pretty much make up anything your heart desires at a moment's notice."

"Thank you but I've just had breakfast," Travis said. "Did you say 'patients'?" he asked, puzzled.

"Yes of course. Do you not know where you are?"

"I saw a flickering hotel sign just off the road. That's why I turned down here."

"Oh that stupid sign…it's acting up again. I keep forgetting to have someone look at it. It didn't say 'hotel', it said 'hospital.'"

"I'm sorry, I didn't realise. I wouldn't have come here if I'd known that."

"Don't worry yourself, honey, we welcome all travellers. You can stay while they repair your car."

"That's kind of you. Maybe I'll just have another coffee," Travis said. As he walked away, he muttered to himself, "This is so bizarre."

####

Nurse Watkins was right. All he did was ask the chef if he could make him some Southern fried chicken wings with fries and coleslaw, and in less than fifteen minutes later, out came what he'd asked for. It wasn't on the buffet table and it wasn't even on the menu. It was something that just popped into his head and he asked for it, even though he'd just gorged on a full breakfast. As soon as he walked into the canteen, he was suddenly hungry again.

It was only after he'd eaten and decided to take a walk around, that he took a good look at his surroundings. It certainly had the appearance of a hospital in some parts of it, but not in all of it. He hadn't noticed the size of the building when he'd come out earlier in the day, but it loomed to the back of the entrance and it seemed that only half of the building was being used. It appeared quite modern in the way it was built, but he'd seen a picture of the same hospital in the lobby that dated back to 1922, and it didn't look all that different. There were a few little differences here and there, but that was all. The front area was solidly built from brick and then insulated to the first level with white wood panels. There were three large, sash style windows with white frames on both sides of the ground floor, that went up another three levels. The entrance jutted out of the building and was made of a mixture of white marble, stone, wood and four Romanesque pillars, two on each side and an open black gate that was firmly bolted to the ground and looked as though it wasn't able to be closed fully anymore. From the front where he had entered the night before, tall thick bushes surrounded the whole property all the way around. The gates at the bottom of the driveway were made of wrought iron with notices that warned people of prosecution if found illegally invading the property. They were closed, whereas the night before, they'd been open—perhaps it was lucky for him that they had been. High metal poles on each side of them held security cameras curiously pointed inwards rather than to see if any visitors had arrived on the outside, but other than that they didn't seem out of place. The building, however, extended maybe an acre back, but it appeared older and less well-kept.

The grounds themselves were beautifully maintained and covered in all sorts of plants. Only an experienced gardener who loved his job would keep them this entirely bug free. Not a spider or web anywhere near them. No greenfly or beetle or in fact, any type of bug, munched on the plants. There were rare desert flowers along the edges of the paths and they displayed all manner of colourful patterns. In the central sections of the gardens, pink apple blossom trees swayed in the breeze and they spilt out their sweet fragrance as he passed them.

Well-kept paths that wound along and then forked out in certain sections of it so that you could walk around the fountain or the gardens in different directions and would then join up again at the other end when the paths would meet and would lead you back inside the building using only the one path. He didn't think it odd that they managed to grow so many plants and flowers and trees while they were still, technically, in the desert.

The patients seemed friendly enough .Some walked around with their IV fluid bags attached to portable IV stands or to belts on their hips. Some looked perfectly healthy and walked around and laughed as if there was nothing wrong with them. Perhaps their illness wasn't as aggressive or maybe they were in recovery and didn't need the equipment?

The inside, on reflection, did look like a hospital—well, it did in certain parts. There were wards and there were several private rooms on each side of the corridors. When he'd arrived there, the porters brought him to a private room so that he wouldn't wake up any of the other patients. He was glad of the peace, there was nothing more frustrating than being tired and surrounded by people snoring or talking in their sleep!

But even though it all seemed to work well and no one seemed distressed, there was something oddly different about the hospital. He couldn't quite put his finger on it, he just had a feeling in the pit of his stomach, that they were hiding something. It didn't smell like a hospital, and the nurses were in uniforms that were different than the ones in the bigger cities, a little bit more old-fashioned—not that it mattered too much.

What mostly was irritating was that soft voice, almost an echo that he couldn't make out. But then again, he thought, it could have just been noise from the traffic on the interstate not that far away.

"Hello," said a voice from behind him. "You're new here?" A young woman, maybe in her middle twenties, extended her hand. "I'm Emma Lou Barnes, but the folks ''round here just call me Emmie."

From her deep accent, Travis could tell she was from somewhere in the Mid-west. As she spoke, her voice just got that little bit higher toward the end of her sentence and it made her last word sound as though she was asking a question rather than ending her conversation.

She was generally quite pretty. The kind of young girl who would take any boy's fancy in some town and who grow up to be the local friendly girl next door. But overall, her skin was an ashen colour as though she hadn't been out in the sun for days. Her eyes were bright green, but slightly bloodshot and her pouty pale pink lips were turned up at the ends which gave her a permanent smile. She wasn't too tall, about five foot four, and below shoulder height to Travis, and thin, she was so painfully thin. Her skin, for the lack of colour, was clear and unblemished and her rosy cheeks only added to accentuate her wavy blonde, rose-coloured hair.

But Travis noticed that her eyes showed the world a different side than that of her beautiful pink lipped smile. They looked sad and lost - even though it was clear from her demeanour, that she wanted people to think she was happy and content. She was fun and vibrant and full of blissful enthusiasm, which made him wonder what was wrong with her and why she was at the hospital.

Travis held out his hand. Her touch was cold, but he shook her hand with a smile. "Travis…my name is Travis."

"Travis? It sure is fine to make your acquaintance, Travis. That's some sweet accent you have there, if you don't mind me saying. Where are you from?"

"Wales," he said with a smile.

"Wales? You'll have to tell me what it's like. I ain't travelled much, and it's nice to hear stories from where some folks come from. Anyhow, welcome to the Desert Springs Hospital for Terminally and Recouper-something-or-other," she said with a grin. "I know I know," she continued with an eye roll. "They couldn't come up with anything more original—or shorter, for that matter. But I guess we are in the desert and somewhere out there, there must be a spring. What are you in for? What's wrong with you?"

Travis smiled. She was a chatterbox, but at least she seemed friendly and entertaining. "Nothing. I'm not in for anything. I was driving along last night and nearly had an accident, I decided to get to the nearest hotel and saw the sign for this place. I thought it said hotel but now I realise it said hospital. It seems half the sign is broken."

"You drove in? Where's your car?" she asked quickly. "Where is it? Do you still have it?"

"One of the porters told me a mechanic came and took it. It's gone for repair, but it should be back later, or tomorrow hopefully. I might go and double check on it in a minute."

"Nah," she said shaking her head. "They've taken it?"

"Yeah, but only for a few repairs and for whatever they can get fixed now on the bodywork and to replace a tyre."

"No," she said sternly, her demeanour not as friendly. "They've taken it. Now you have no way of leaving here." She looked around her and lowered her voice. "You don't know what you've wandered into. Were you sick before you came here?"

"No, I said I'm not sick," Travis said, puzzled. "And I'm not stuck here. I'm leaving as soon as the car is ready. Tonight, if that's possible."

She looked around. Two burly male nurses were making their way over to them. They were walking fast, almost running. Emmie's cheerful face had changed. Her smile was gone and she looked anxious as she took a few steps away from him. "I'll make sure to catch you later, Travis," she said and with that, she turned around quickly. The nurses sideswiped Travis and headed off in quick pursuit of Emmie.

Travis couldn't help but think about what Emmie had said to him, "Now you have no way of leaving," and thought he should go find Nurse Watkins and see what the situation was with the car. He walked into the hospital and straight over to the reception area.

The frosted glass panel was closed as he approached the reception desk. When he tapped it, the glass panel quickly opened with a hard swish to the side that shook the counter. The stern-looking nurse behind it peered out as though he had disturbed something very important. "Hi, I'm looking for Nurse Watkins."

Her thin pinched lips sneered as she bellowed, "Go back to your room!"

"What? No…I'm not a patient here, I arrived last night. I…"

"Who are you then? What do you want with her?"

"I-I'm Travis Williams," he stuttered slightly. "She had my car taken away to be fixed. I want to know when it's coming back."

She turned her whole body and looked at her colleague who was sat at a desk, and then back to Travis. "Well I don't know, do I?" she said sharply. "You'll have to ask her."

"That's what I'm trying to do. Do you know where she is?"

"She don't like being disturbed at this time of the day, don't you go bothering her. You'll have to wait until this evening."

"I'm hoping to be gone by this evening if they've managed to fix the car. Just call her, she'll be fine, she knows I'm waiting to leave."

The nurse and her colleague gave a slight laugh. "Leave?" and then she closed the glass panel in front of him. Behind the panel, he could hear both nurses laugh. "He thinks he's just gonna walk out of here? Just like that!" Then they broke into hysterical laughter. So much for patient care, he thought. He'd go find her himself.

As Travis began to walk back down the corridor, the sound of a bell rang five times in short five second bursts, through the loud speaker. People started to walk out of the wards and their rooms and some came in from the gardens. It was already early evening and as they all shuffled toward the canteen, he found himself in the midst of the crowd and pushed that way too. He stopped walking as soon as he passed the clock and saw that it was six o'clock. How could the day have passed so quickly?

The patients each sat in the exact same seats as he'd seen them in at breakfast. Not one deviated to make things different. Even Travis was drawn to the same seat as the night he'd arrived and soon the other patients sat around him. He looked 'round, hoping to see Emmie, but he couldn't see her. "Do any of you know where Emmie is?" he asked. But none of the other five men that sat around the table even looked up at him. "Short, blonde, doesn't stop talking?" he added. No replies. Travis shrugged. "Guess not, then."

The kitchen staff came out from the back of the canteen and placed plain white soup dishes in front of each patient and then spooned out two ladles into each bowl from a cauldron that they wheeled around on a portable tea trolley. No one touched it. The patients made no attempts to move, except for Travis who grabbed a roll from the centre of the basket on their table, broke it in half and dipped it into the hot soup. Then a short whistle sounded and each patient lifted up their spoons and began to eat. It was almost robotic — spoon in, up to the mouth, back to the bowl, in almost perfect synchronicity.

Travis peered over his spoon and looked around the canteen, but no one spoke a word, and they didn't make a sound. It wasn't an extremely big canteen. It had around twenty tables that could accommodate six people at each. But only ten of the tables were occupied. There was a long counter with stacked dinner plates, cups and saucers and a cold drinks dispenser with paper cups on a tray alongside it. Even though food was laid out on separate counters and staff stood behind them, no one made an attempt to get up and get anything. Behind the counter, there were two swinging doors that led into the kitchen area, but all that Travis could see inside the kitchen were a few metal tray trolleys and that was only whenever anyone would come out or go back in. It was as he would expect in a hospital — clean, sterile and painted white with light purple coving on the edges of the ceiling. There were a few pictures on the walls, but nothing too bright or modern or interesting. For a room full of patients, there wasn't even the sound of spoons hitting the china bowls. Then, almost at the same time, patients placed their spoons alongside the bowls. The kitchen staff collected them and replaced them with another plate and more food. As before, the patients didn't touch it until the whistle sounded. Travis couldn't help but stare at the patients as he shovelled the sautéed potatoes into his mouth. If anything, the food was good, hot and plentiful. But there was no eye contact with anyone, no chatter, no one asked how the other was feeling, as though they weren't allowed. When that food was finished, the plates were quickly cleared and a pre-plated dessert placed down in front of them all and the whistle sounded again. And as soon as that course was finished, it was collected too. The next time the bell sounded, just four rings this time, the patients got up, turned away from the tables and walked away to leave the kitchen staff to clean up. Travis wondered what the hell was going on.

Nurse Watkins' office wasn't too far from the canteen, so Travis walked over in the hopes he could catch her before she disappeared again. The day was almost over and he was another day off his schedule, so he was even more eager for news of the car.

He knocked on the door and didn't wait for a response from inside, he just marched in. But it was empty. The sound of a voice behind him, made him jump. "She's not in there."

Travis turned to see one of the male porters who had chased after Emmie in the gardens earlier that day, standing behind him with a patient in a wheelchair. "She'll be doing the rounds at this time. Some of the patients are very old and have been with us for a while. She's just making sure they ain't dead." He laughed as he pushed the chair away and continued down the corridor. Travis raised an eyebrow. Well this was certainly different to the NHS back home. But he had to find her and get out of this place. He followed the porter down the corridor but as he turned the corner, the porter was gone! There weren't any other private rooms on that corridor and the ward was farther down, so where had he gone? Travis walked on and saw the lift. Maybe Nurse Watkins was up on the next floor? He waited for the lift to come down and as soon as it arrived, and the doors opened, he got in. He pressed the button for the second floor, but it didn't move and he couldn't hear any of the machinery working. He pressed the button again and then again, and then punched it hard with his closed fist a third time, until it finally moved

On the second floor, the doors opened and Travis heard the familiar southern twang of Nurse Watkins' voice bellow out as he got out of the lift and walked over to the ward. She was ticking off a nurse when she looked up, "Hello Travis, how are you feeling today?"

"I'm fine. Why is everyone concerned with how I feel?" He wasn't in the mood for pleasantries now, he just wanted to leave.

"That's just the way we are. It's polite to ask you know? Is something wrong? What's bothering you?"

"What's bothering me is that I've been looking for you for most of the day. I want to know when my car is coming back, so I can get back on the road."

"Well that's hardly my fault if you haven't been able to find me. I do have a lot of other patients to look after, so I'm busy all the time. And it hasn't been most of the day because you've been asleep for half of it," she said in a cross voice. "Now what's this about your car? I don't understand," she said, abruptly.

"You don't understand what?" If she was going to give him attitude, then he would return it with a harsh response.

"I don't understand what car you're on about?"

"My car!" He said. "The car I came in last night. The car you had taken away for repair."

"Travis, you didn't come here last night."

"What are you talking about?"

"It wasn't last night," she said softly. "You did not arrive last night."

"Yes I did. I drove in here last night. Don't you remember? You were at the entrance."

"Yes, I remember when you arrived, but you were brought here, you didn't drive here yourself."

"What do you mean I didn't drive here? Are you insane? We spoke about the state of the car only this morning…you were going to get someone to look at it."

"We never had that conversation, Travis."

"We did. It was only this morning!"

"Travis, you've been here for five days. When you were brought to us, you were drifting in and out of consciousness and you've been asleep for three of those days. You woke up yesterday. Or actually, you woke up the night before for a little while, but then you went back to sleep again."

"What?"

Nurse Watkins inhaled and then began. "You had a concussion when the police found you on the side of the road. You were in an accident and they took you to the local hospital. But they couldn't care for you there, so you were brought here."

"No they didn't. I drove. Now look, all you have to do is call the garage and get the car back here. I don't care what state it's in. I don't care if the police pull me over, just get it here. Or call me a cab so I can get to the next town and hire another car."

"You can't leave here just yet. You're not well. The doctor says you have swelling on the brain and until that goes down, you have to be monitored. I wouldn't worry too much about those bruises." She gestured around her own face. "They'll be gone soon enough, they don't look as bad anymore."

"What bruises?" Travis looked around for anything that would give him his reflection, but saw nothing. "And there's nothing wrong with my head!" He yelled. The same time that he spoke, he prodded his head hard to prove a point and then grimaced. It was like he'd stuck a needle into his head.

"Hurts, right?" said Nurse Watkins. "Let me take you back to your room. It might be a good idea for you to get an early night."

Travis stared at her for a moment. What was going on? His head did hurt when he touched it, but the accident? He'd escaped it without a scratch. He tried to remember, but his brain was blank.

"You're telling me that I was 'brought' here?"

"Yes," she replied softly. "Now let's get you back to your room."

CHAPTER THREE

Travis lay in the bed and tried to comprehend what was happening to him. Part of him wanted to scream and shout and run out of the building, and yet another part of him felt very at ease at the explanation she'd given him, like he was accepting it. But he knew he was fine—he'd dodged the accident.

Then why did he have that bump on his head?

He'd driven himself to the hospital, he remembered the neon sign, but…but then he could also remember the back of a drivers' head too. Where did that come from?

He remembered the road as he turned into it, and the neon sign.

But did he?

And what did Nurse Watkins mean when she said he'd been there for a week already? He got up and went into the bathroom to splash water onto his face. He looked at his reflection in the small shaving mirror and saw half his face was covered in nasty shades of blues and purples. Then he parted the side of his hair, and saw a large gash with small stitches. He pushed himself away from the wash basin and looked around the room. He could feel his heart pound in his chest, his head became light and he swayed slightly.

What was going on?

He'd missed that accident—he'd missed it.

What was wrong with him? Why couldn't he remember anything else? He marched out of the bathroom. He packed what he could into his rucksack and walked out of the room. He'd walk or drag himself to the next town, if he had to.

Down the corridor, he approached the door of the heavy glass security partition and reached for the handle. It was locked. He tapped on the glass and then pounded on it. It was resilient enough to withstand a strong punch. He turned and walked the other way—he knew there was a nurse's station down there because he'd passed it earlier. But as he got closer, he saw that there was no sign of anyone at the desk.

A sudden noise, made him turn around.

One of the patients had left his room and was walking over to him. Travis let out a feeble scream as the man, who was in a near catatonic state, got closer. His grey complexion shimmered in the lights of the corridor. His eyes were sunken and grey and his bald head was bent over to the side as he stared at Travis. His feet shuffled on the tiles of the hospital floor as he walked toward Travis. The patient seemed determined to get close to him. His arms were outstretched and his long, thin fingers moved quickly in an attempt to snare him. If Travis could pick any horror genre that he hated above all else, it would be zombies, and this patient was just too close to the real thing.

Travis took a quick sidestep and held out his arms to stop the patient from getting too close. He jumped aside and got around him with the agility of a trained gymnast, headed back to his own room, closed the door and propped up a chair under the handle to make sure no one could get in.

The sudden appearance of lights from outside his window illuminated his room and he turned around to see what was going on. Strong floodlights in the gardens gave the night a day glow and Travis saw twelve patients walking in formation. Their feet shuffled through the gravel on the path in a line of three as they marched over to the fountain. They wore long light-blue bed gowns and black slippers, but their appearance was even more disturbing and even more frightening than that of the patient in the corridor. These patients could hardly stand. It was as though they were being held up by an invisible rope. They all shuffled slowly behind two nurses. One behind the other, their expressionless faces just stared ahead and their dark-rimmed eyes were wide open. The nurse at the front shouted, "Walk!" and they followed. After a few short paces, another shouted, "Stop!" and they stopped immediately.

The nurses talked amongst themselves until the one nurse again yelled, "Walk!" and off they went again.

He hadn't noticed these people in the dining room, so where had they come from?

And that nagging voice that it appeared no-one else could hear, was back. Like a whisper, but still loud enough to bother him, the voice wasn't coming from outside his room because other than that single patient, there was no one else out there. He put his head next to an air vent to hear if the voices came from the other floors and were just filtering down. But it seemed that the voices were only coming from inside his room. Travis thought for a moment. Perhaps there was an old speaker hidden somewhere in the walls that hadn't been removed when the hospital was refurbished last time? Maybe it used to pipe in music to relax people while they slept and it was still working?

Perhaps it was turning too quickly that did it. It could have been one of many things - the shock of seeing that zombie patient or even the sight of the other patients outside in the gardens or even taking in what Nurse Watkins had told him, but he suddenly felt light-headed and weak and had to lie down on the bed.

Sleep came too quickly and the dream that he fell into unsettled him, making him toss and turn. In the dream, he joined the patients outside to walk around the fountain. He heard the voice from the nurse at the front and her command to "Walk!" and then they all began to move in slow motion. Then he noticed his hands. They glowed in a shadowy hallucinogenic haze of bright colours. Even his clothes had changed. He was dressed in the same hospital gown and slippers as they were. A splinter group of patients walked in the opposite direction toward him, like the ensemble of a marching band performing a routine. Every one of them stared down at the floor as they shuffled past him and avoided hitting not only him, but the others that walked the same direction as him. Travis tried to stop walking, but couldn't, he had no control over his actions.

A group of five nurses watched them all as they just walked around and around. The nurses' laughter turned to high-pitched hysterics as the five of them began to sway from side to side in manic dreamlike postures. Their eyes bulged and stared out, their faces distorted. Their smiles grew bigger and bigger, outgrowing their own faces. Their skin changed colour and their bodies shrivelled and became smaller and hunchbacked.

Then, out of the corner of his eye, Travis spotted Emmie and could suddenly move freely. He managed to push past all those in front of him to get to her. "Emmie!" he shouted and touched the back of her shoulder. "I've been looking for you all day." She turned her head slightly to look at him and he saw her eyes, sunken and black, no expression, no life, as pale as all the others and with no recognition of who he was. She had four small red patches on the side of her head similar to burn marks. And then she turned her head back around, stared straight ahead again and joined the others on their walk. Travis held back a little, but again found that he couldn't stop walking. Emmie was already a few patients away from him and he was back in the same line of the crowd that he had started with. And as hard as he tried to stop walking, he just couldn't.

Travis woke and realised it was morning again, and even more bizarre, he was wearing hospital pyjamas, whereas he'd gone to bed the night before fully dressed?

CHAPTER FOUR

If seeing that patient wasn't enough to do it, his nightmare made him even more determined to get the hell out of there!

Car or no car, or whatever story Nurse Watkins had made up, bruises and bumps, there was nothing else physically wrong with him. He could get up and walk around - he was eating, drinking and talking. It was time to leave. He'd sign all waivers and take whatever the consequences.

The other patients were also up and were taking a walk around the wards and corridors outside of his room, he could even hear their chatter from the gardens. The porters talked loudly and laughed as they passed his door and called out to some of the other patients. He opened his door and came face to face with one of the younger nurses.

"Hello, sleepyhead," she said with a smile. "I was wondering if I was going to have to come in and wake you again today."

"Why? What time is it?"

"It's almost 11:30, you've missed breakfast this morning but I'm sure we can find you something if you're hungry and don't want to wait until lunch. And you haven't taken any of your medications yet either. I'll go and get them."

"What medication?"

"You know exactly what medication, you've been taking them since you arrived."

"No I haven't." argued Travis.

"Do I have to get Nurse Watkins?" said the nurse quietly, "do you need me to bring her over again?" She stepped closer and whispered, "You know what happened last time?"

"No…I…"

An elderly patient interrupted them with a smile as he walked nearby. "You look a lot perkier this morning." His broad Southern accent bellowed in the corridor. He tapped his forehead in a mock military salute. "We was wondering if you'd venture out of your room. Emmie told us you were newly awake."

"I'll be right back," the nurse said.

"Emmie!" Travis said quickly to the old man and

ignoring the nurse. "Where is she?"

"Yeah, sweet young thing. She keeps us all peppy. Got to say, she definitely gives me a spring in my old step. Some of the other women here, well, they're not too friendly and some days, you just need a pretty face to brighten up the day."

"I need to speak to her."

"Well you can try the gardens around the back—she does like to take a walk around there and smell those flowers. Or maybe try the games room, some days she likes to play checkers with the trancers—they don't argue when she cheats!"

"Trancers?"

"Well that's what we call 'em… those who are not quite with us. You'll know what I mean when you see 'em."

Travis tried the games room first as it was the closest. Almost immediately after he entered, some of the patients seemed anxious to be near him.

"So young," said one elderly woman as she unexpectedly stroked his face with the back of her hand.

It made him flinch and bump straight into another patient.

"The voices," said the other patient, looking straight at Travis. "Have you heard them voices? They be different for all of us, y'know." Then he walked away repeating the words, "Different for all of us."

Then another patient crept up beside him and whispered in his ear, "Escape is within you." And she walked away without a glance back.

He looked across the room to three tables with checkerboards laid out and with the pieces placed on squares that mimicked a game in progress. Two men sat in a comatose state staring at each other. Were they the trancers? So the man he'd seen last night in the corridor and those he'd seen in the gardens and those he'd dreamt about, were trancers? But how could he dream about people he knew nothing about? Travis stared at them for a brief moment. They all had an albino appearance with deep dark ridges around the eyes. But these trancers were dressed in pale green hospital pyjamas and black slippers, instead of the long nightgowns in his dream. Their hands were on the table, palms down and they sat up straight. He was walking past them to get to the window, when suddenly one came to life and grabbed his hand. He jumped and almost screamed out loud.

"No escape," the man said without looking up. "Can't get out." His sharp nails dug into Travis's hand and scratched him as Travis pulled back to get away from him.

The other man tilted his head to the side, shouted, "Run!" And then grinned as he turned his head back. Both men went back into their trancer stare as though nothing had been said or done.

Startled, Travis turned and quickly walked out. His breath was shallow as he made his way down the corridor. What the hell. He was getting out of here now.

He was very nearly out of the building, when Emmie walked in.

"Hey stranger, where've you been hiding?"

"I've just... they..." He pointed down the corridor and then stopped. He calmed himself down. The trancers had spooked him that was all. No need to show the girl he was a wimp. "I've been looking for you and no one could tell me where you were."

"I've been around," she said with a smile. "Why don't we take a walk? The air is really warm today."

As they walked away, Travis noticed four small red marks on the side of her forehead.

"What are those?" he pointed to the marks.

She touched them gently. "Oh these. I don't know what they are. They appear every few weeks. I just remember having a bad headache and then I wake up and there they are. I don't always feel right, about the same time they happen, so I keep to my room out of sight and the quiet helps. That's why you ain't seen me for a few days."

"A few days? But I saw you yesterday."

"No honey, you didn't. You saw me a few days ago. Y'all been in your room alone too. But I hears ya. I know"—she sighed and then smiled—"that sometimes the days here go by too quickly. Before you know it—"

"I've only been here two days," he interrupted, correcting her. Then he thought for a moment. "No, it's been three days. It's been three days since I got here."

"Honey, you bin here for longer than that. You bin here...goodness, it must be two weeks maybe. An' then you bin asleep for more than half of it. Time, it goes too damn quick here for some things and then it drags for others."

He shook his head. Maybe she was just confused.

"But it ain't all bad here," she continued. "The food is good. Y'know all I have to do is think about what it is I want to eat and then there it is. It's as if they can read my mind. But then, I've always thought that it's possible to do that. Y'know, to control what you're thinking. And if that's true, then you can also control what happens here too." She smiled and touched her forehead. "But I reckon it'd take someone real strong to do that. Y'know, change things with their mind."

Travis smiled and nodded politely. Maybe that's what was wrong with her. She wasn't too right in the head. He let her ramblings go. "How come you ended up here?" he asked.

"Well see, I was driving along minding my own business one evening. I remember the night sky was so pretty and I could smell something real sweet in the air like the bluebells and the jasmine flowers that grow next to a creek outside of town. Then, the next minute, I wake up here. Thing is, I'm from a town near Louisiana, it's way out back in the country and you'd never even know it was there unless you happen on it by accident... And this hospital? Well, we're out in the desert and I know this ain't near my home."

"Didn't you ever ask why you were sent here, away from your home?"

"Well, see here...I was a bit confused about that at the start. But Nurse Watkins, she explained it all to me and I didn't feel so sad afterwards. But I sure do miss my folks and my sisters, even though we used to argue all the time. I miss them."

"Why don't they visit you?"

"Ain't allowed."

"Why?"

"Well, Nurse Watkins says it'd not help my recovery to be all sad when they leave. It's not too bad here. You get used to it, you get used to the rules. And then new people join us and it's nice to meet different folks and hear about where they come from."

"Well I don't think it's that good here. No one answers your questions, and they keep you all overmedicated." He placed his hands over his ears. "And that music. It plays all day, every day. It used to be one of my favourite songs, but now I never want to hear it again."

"There ain't no music playing, darling," she said and raised an eyebrow. "I wouldn't mind a bit of music being played in my head, some days the silence is—"

"There is, can't you hear it?" Travis interrupted. "It's not very loud right now, but it's there."

"Maybe after my accident, something happened and I don't hear as well as I did before it."

"Accident? You didn't mention you'd had an accident."

"I don't remember it...well, I don't remember much of it anyhow. I was driving a dirt road near the creek, not far from where I live. I been driving that same road since…hell, it's been years. I can remember bits of that day, you know, like a dream but you don't know if it's real or not? And then next thing I remember is waking up here. Heck, these days I don't even remember how long I been here."

"Like me, then," he joked.

"Like most of us." Emmie turned to see some of

the patients walking along the garden pathway.

"Emmie, I don't know what's going on here, but I know something's not right. I'm leaving here today and I don't think you should stay here either. Come with me."

"There ain't no leaving here, Travis, ain't you been told that yet? Anyway, didn't you say they took your car?"

"We can walk...run even! This place, Emmie, it's not like a proper hospital. No one comes to visit. There's nothing wrong with some patients, like you and me, and some others are… well, they are 'trancers'. They should be in a different hospital."

"They're the only things here that scare me," Emmie said. "When you look at them, it's like their bodies are still here, breathing an' all, but their souls have long gone. Do you think folks with no souls look like that?"

"I don't know," he said. "I've never thought about it. Why do they all look alike? Why are they only men?"

"They're not just men, Travis, there's women in there too. That's why it just creeps me out some days. I hope we don't all end up like that."

"Not if we get out of here first. I can't stand it anymore—the nightmares, this music in my head, those trancers, even Nurse Watkins. I want out and I want it now."

"Travis, don't you go and stress yourself out. If you do, it takes over you and—"

But her warning came too late. Travis had already passed out and was lying on the floor.

CHAPTER FIVE

It was like déjà vu. Travis wasn't amused.

That same annoying music and the muffled voices woke him from his sleep. His head really hurt and his back ached and he couldn't quite remember what had happened or why and how he got back to his room. He looked over to the window and saw it was night. The moon looked bigger and brighter than Travis had ever seen it before. Maybe it was being out in the desert without any city lights to pollute the skies, but it lit up his room. All was quiet—apart from the same music and the voices that still, apparently, no one else could hear.

And then an overwhelming sense of frustration and anger came over him. This afternoon, he'd made a determined effort to leave this so-called hospital and…and then he remembered he'd been talking to Emmie. He heard her say that he shouldn't stress himself out and then... Bam! Concrete floor.

He got out of bed and even though he could hardly focus on what was in front of him, and with his head continuing its tumultuous spin, he was determined to find out what was really going on there. Why was everyone so cryptic? He opened the door and crept out. He looked both ways to make sure no one was around and immediately saw that the glass barrier and its doors were open. He quickly headed toward it and through to the other side. He hadn't been able to get to this side of the hospital before, but if there was a door to the outside world at this end of it that no one was watching, then he was taking it.

The room doors on this side of the corridor looked more like cells as he passed them. As he walked by one of them, a high pitched shriek made him look into the room through the small open slit in the door. Inside the room, a patient sat bolt upright on a bed, not quite a trancer, but he didn't look far from being one. He was as deathly pale as the others were. He was aged, in his fifties or maybe slightly older, it was hard to tell. His hair was grey and brushed back and he had small patches of black/grey facial hair on his chin and face. He sobbed and moaned as he rocked back and forth. Travis couldn't quite make out what he was saying, so he pressed his ear to the opening to try to catch a few of the words. The man looked over to Travis and made a charge for the door. He screamed and kicked at the door to try to get it open. Travis closed the flap in the door, stepped away quickly, and hoped that no one could hear the screams coming from inside.

He looked left and saw a hand coming out of the opening of the room next door. The slot was slightly bigger than in the previous door. Another male patient gestured for him to get closer. "Where are you going?" he whispered. His voice was deep as he tried to catch his breath with every word that he spoke. "No getting out from here you know? I tried it, I tried it."

Travis stepped away from the door, and the man turned and walked back to his bed and got in it. "No getting out, they got eyes everywhere!" he shouted toward Travis. "No getting out."

Travis could still hear him shout as he made his way quickly down the corridor again. There was a stairwell just within his reach, until a porter stepped in front of him and blocked him from it. "Are you going somewhere?"

"Yes," Travis said. "I'm leaving."

"Why do you want to leave?"

"I came here because I was lost," Travis replied as he tried to barge past him.

"We are all lost, in our own way."

"No, I meant I was driving and I was tired and I took a turn down a road where I thought there was a sign that said hotel, but instead I ended up here."

"I remember you. I brought you in when you arrived."

"I don't remember seeing you," Travis said, taking a step back.

"Of course you wouldn't. You were pretty much out of it."

"For the last time, did Nurse Watkins tell you all to keep to this story? I drove here. I pulled up outside this place and Nurse Watkins was at the door."

"She's always at the door when new patients arrive. That's her job, to bring you all in."

"I'm not a new patient and I wasn't arriving. Why doesn't anyone understand that? Are any of you even listening to me?"

"You're still confused. Let's get you back to your

room." The porter reached out to grab Travis's arm, but he pulled it away.

"Get out of my way!" he said as he pushed the porter aside, "I'm not staying here another night."

Two more porters grabbed hold of Travis and pulled him back from the stairwell door. As much as he struggled and fought, there was no way he could win against three burly men. They dragged him back down the corridor, threw him into his room and locked the door behind them.

Travis banged on the door. "You can't lock this door!" he shouted. "Let me out, I'm not supposed to be in here."

One of the porters shouted back. "We'll unlock it in the morning. Go back to bed!"

The music started again. This time, it was louder than before and it filled his head until he couldn't concentrate on what was going on outside of the room anymore. "Not now!" he yelled as he placed his hands over his ears. "It's driving me crazy." Then he stopped yelling. The music had become quieter and a voice replaced it instead. "What?" Someone had called out his name. Even with the music and his hands over his ears, he heard it. "Is someone else in here?" He heard the voices again, but this time there were a few of them. They were talking to each other and then he heard a softer laugh. It was clearly female. Then the music played again and drowned the voices out. Travis felt his stomach turn, his chest hurt and he began to shake. He couldn't catch his breath. His fingers tingled and his knees buckled from under him. He was going to fall. He threw himself on the bed and covered his head with his pillow. He didn't want to hear the music again because when he did, he would… Minutes later, he fell asleep.

Bright blue flashing lights woke Travis and he got up to see what was going on outside his room. He looked at his reflection and saw that he was fully dressed. He didn't remember getting dressed. He'd gone to bed in the pyjamas the hospital had provided. Had he blacked out again? He couldn't remember what he was doing before he went to sleep. Nonetheless, he found himself walking down the corridor again. The lights flashed around him, like emergency lights when an alarm goes off. It sent a swirl of intense patterns around the corridor that highlighted the doors he'd passed earlier, before the porters stopped him from going any farther. But even so, the corridor was silent. No one was walking, running or doing anything. He was totally alone.

He took a step closer to the first door and cautiously looked inside, but the room was empty. He moved gingerly over to the second room and pressed his face up against the door, where he saw a rather large nurse and a scrawny patient in the middle of having sex. Whereas the man was naked, she was in her uniform with just her pants in her hand. She stopped in semi pump and turned her head. Her eyes were like all the others, black and sunken, no life in them. Travis gasped as he saw her face distort in front of him, her smile grew and changed to a dark swirl in the middle of her face that made her unrecognisable. The male patient lay motionless under her, she initiated all the moves and he was simply her plaything. His face was pale, his expressionless eyes bulged, his mouth open while his lips were cracked and bloody red. But Travis knew him. When he'd last seen this man, he'd moved freely around his room and around the wards. Now he looked just like the trancers he'd met in the games room. The nurse turned back around and carried on pumping on top of him as Travis moved away from the door.

He was almost apprehensive as he passed another door and he peered inside of it. A patient stood naked in the middle of that room with a large serrated knife in his hand. As soon as he saw Travis at the door, he plunged the knife into his own chest over and over. Blood gushed down his body from the open wounds and severed arteries that spilt out over the floor and splattered over the walls. The patient laughed as he stared at Travis. Then for a moment, he stopped, smiled at him and then plunged the knife deep into his throat. The trapped blood in his larynx gurgled as he shrieked with laughter that made the red liquid squirt over the walls to the side of him.

Travis ran down the corridor, he looked at the other doors as he passed them but avoided looking into them. He could hear noises from behind each one of the doors but couldn't bring himself to look. He reached the same stairwell that he'd been stopped at earlier. He opened the door and ran down the stairs as fast as he could. He took two steps at a time and almost tripped over his own feet to reach the bottom even faster.

But something was wrong. He looked down the centre of the stairwell to see that he was at least three levels up, but the floor he'd started on was only one level up from the ground floor. Even so, it seemed that as soon as he reached the bottom of that level, another appeared underneath it to keep him always three levels up. Out of breath, he stopped. This was no good, so he pulled open the door of the level he'd just left, and found himself back on his own floor, two flights down from the stairs he was running down. Travis stopped as he took everything in. "What the hell?" It made no sense. He turned back and into the stairway and took each step down slower this time. To his relief, this time, he made it onto the next level, so he opened the door and walked in. It was quiet and cold and he shivered as he entered. Ice smothered the walls and a grey/blue mist floated on the ground. It certainly wasn't this cold in the stairway or on his floor. He needed to find Emmie because they both didn't deserve to be there, but he didn't know which door was her room. He could see his breath as he slowly walked to the first door and apprehensively looked inside. A man lay still on the bed. Travis couldn't tell if he was breathing or not, he was so still and quiet. Another trancer, perhaps? He walked on and looked inside the next room and another man sat naked and cross-legged on his bed with his eyes closed. Blue and frozen, the man opened his black eyes and stared at Travis with a wide toothy grin. A small reflex hammer lay on the bed next to him and the man looked down at it and then picked it up and hit himself in the face. Sections of his frozen cheek fell onto the bed and then bounced off it to the floor. He hit himself again…and then again…to expose his skull and cheekbones. And he continued to hammer, but this time even harder into his chest and his ribs. Pieces flew off and hurtled themselves across the room with the force of the hits. Travis pushed himself away from the door. He could feel his heart race, it pulsated fast and so hard that he thought it would just burst out of his chest and now his head was dizzy too. This wasn't the time for him to black out!

He moved on to the next door and saw Emmie

lying on the bed. As with the others, she looked dead. He couldn't tell if there was any movement from her chest to suggest that there were any signs of life in her. Travis pushed at her door, but it wouldn't open. He shoved his whole body into it. He pushed at it, took a step back and pushed harder until the ice seal around it cracked and it began to give way. It then burst open and collided into the wall behind it. Flakes of ice that filled the entire room fell to the floor from the ceiling and walls and narrowly missed him as he rushed over to her bed. But she was dead. Travis's heart sank. How could she be dead? It wasn't possible. What had they done to her? To everyone on that ward?

And just when he thought the whole nightmare couldn't get any worse, her hand touched his. He bolted to the other side of the room. "W-what? B-but you're so cold! How…"

"You're dreaming, Travis," she whispered with a smile. "It's all a nightmare. There's no escape from here, we've all told you. We've all tried to tell you over and over…" her voice trailed away. She tilted her head to the right and held out her hand, "This is how we truly are."

"I'm not dreaming! This is real," Travis said, confused. "What's happen—" He blacked out before he could finish his question.

CHAPTER SIX

Travis woke up in his room again. Apprehensively, he took a few steps toward the door, took a deep breath and then walked out of his room, not knowing who or what he would bump into this time. That whole night had been another shocker. Was what he'd experienced last night a nightmare? He couldn't tell whether it was or not. But it had to have just been one, because everything looked normal again. He hoped to not bump into anyone and was about to make for the stairs again when he heard a voice.

"Checkers!" a high-pitched voice from behind startled him. "Do you play checkers?"

Travis turned around to see Emmie with a huge smile on her face. She was wearing a pretty blue flowery dress that came to just above her knees and her hair was up in a ponytail with a few side stragglers making it look casual, but still attractive. "Huh?" he asked, confused.

"My, you look like you've seen a ghost," she said in a concerned tone of voice. "Are you sure you should be up and walking around?"

"No…no, I'm fine."

"It don't look like you're fine."

"I'm OK, really." He took a breath, and tried to get the image of the last time he'd seen her out of his head. He wanted to make sense from it before he sounded like a lunatic. "It doesn't matter. It's probably nothing." He looked at her smile. It seemed different. Or maybe it was still the mental image he had, depending on the state of his mind right now. "Checkers? That's like draughts, right?"

"No, it's like checkers. I don't know what that other one is."

"It's what we call the game back home. Yes I play, and I'm good at it too, just to warn you."

"I bet you ain't played it as long as I have," Emmie teased. "You want to play in the games room or shall we play in the garden?"

"Why don't we take it outside? We can get some air and be away from listening ears."

"Listening ears? Oh, you're so funny," Emmie said. "I'll go get the board and you can meet me by the fountain."

A few minutes later, Emmie ran into the gardens with a board under her arm and a box in her hands. She almost slid along the grass as she sat in front of Travis and opened up the board and the box. "You want black or white?" she asked.

"Black," Travis said and leaned into her with a smile. "To match my black soul."

Emmie snorted and pointed at him, "You are a wicked one," she teased. "I see I'm gonna have to keep a close eye on you. You're a heap of trouble, I can see it."

"You have no idea." Travis laughed. "Now checkers, it really is like draughts."

"Well I ain't never heard of draughts, unless you're talking about the wind coming in through old windows." She chuckled. "I don't know what it's like."

"Black jumps white and takes the piece? And when my black piece gets on your white side of the board, I become the King?"

"When your piece? Well buddy, let's just see about that. But I think it's only fair to warn you, I'm really good at this game. I don't get beat too easily," Emmie said as she placed her pieces on the board.

"That's because you haven't played against me. And besides, you only play the trancers and that's why you always win."

"Whaa--" Emmie said, astonished. "Well, let's just start this game and see, shall we?"

Emmie made the first move, followed by Travis, then Emmie again. He smiled when he saw her eyes widen when she thought he'd made a bad move. She was already two steps ahead of him in her head it appeared by the look on her face, but he was three ahead of her.

"Travis, tell me about where you come from," Emmie said. "Is it pretty?"

Travis took a moment before he answered, then smiled and said, "It's beautiful. You know, it's funny you never realise any of that until you are far away from it."

"Yeah I hear you. I miss home too." She laughed. "Tell me about yours. Tell me what it's like."

"Well I live just outside a capital city called Cardiff. It's not too far to be away from all the fun, but just far enough out to leave the madness of city life. I work in the city during the week, so it's nice to get out away from it all."

"I've never really been to any big city. I've been to St. Louis once when I was a young 'un. I can still remember all the folks rushing about and all the shops and pretty clothes in the window."

"Well Cardiff is a lot like that. It's big and busy with cars and buses everywhere and people rushing about like they should have been wherever they were going five minutes before." He laughed. "But the town I live in, is called Brynteifi."

"Er, what?" Emmie raised an eyebrow.

"It's a Welsh name. Wales has its own language too, although I don't speak it. Lots of my friends do. Bryn-teifi" He broke the word down into two syllables. "Bryn, like B.r.i.n."

"Brin..." Emmie began.

"Teifi. Like Tay and vee."

"Brin-tay-vee!" she exclaimed.

"That's it. You got it."

Emmie gave a little jump and clap "Yee-ayy."

"Anyway, there's not much there, which is why I work in Cardiff. My parents still live there and I visit them every Sunday for a family dinner. I don't live too far from them, in a flat."

"In a flat? In a flat what?" Emmie asked.

"Oh no, not a flat anything." Travis laughed. "A flat is what we call an apartment."

"Brynteifi has chapels, small shops and factories. The town is surrounded by mountains and thick woods with tall trees. In the winter, you can tell when it's going to rain, because it hits all of that first and we can see it coming in. A bit later, we get the rain."

"Like a tornado warning? We have them too. If the birds fly high and away, if the wind feels damp, then we know to bunk down for a storm."

"Yes, like that. Guess us locals know the signs, right?"

"Yep, that we do." She nodded. "What else is there?"

"Well, past the mountains and into some valleys, there are waterfalls, caves and old castles."

Emmie's face began to change. Travis saw that she was sad and almost teary. "What's wrong?"

"I'm never going to see those places, am I?" she said sadly.

"Why not? You can still travel when you leave here. You can get on a plane and just go. Anywhere you want."

"I've never been on a plane. Never been close to one, either. But I can close my eyes and be in all those places without leaving my room," she said, suddenly cheerful again.

"Emmie, have you ever tried to leave here? I mean, just tell them you were OK and you were discharging yourself?"

"Why would I do that when I'm still sick?" She moved her piece closer to his. Travis noticed her eyes widen even more - she would be rubbish at poker.

"But you're not sick. Look at you, walking and talking." He looked down on the board and moved his piece away from her next move. That made her frown. "You're here playing draughts… sorry, checkers," he corrected himself, "with me and you don't seem sick.

Have you thought that maybe they are keeping you here against your will? Like a prisoner, instead of a patient? Experimenting on you?" He pointed at the red marks on the side of her forehead.

Emmie looked up at him. "No, I haven't thought about leaving and you're wrong, I am sick." She touched her head. "I'm sick in here, that's why I have the marks."

"Haven't you even tried to leave or asked to go somewhere else?"

"Why would I go somewhere else? They all know me here. The folks are real friendly and the food is good and I like this hospital. It has everything I want, when I want it."

"Except freedom and visits from the people you love—your family and your friends. I don't buy that it would upset you when you have to say goodbye to them when they leave. I think it would speed things up for lots of you."

Emmie wasn't smiling anymore. "You don't like it here, do you?"

"It's not that. It's just that…"

"Don't you like being here with us or with me?"

Her voice was slightly raised and it was no longer that cheerful tone that he found comforting.

"No I didn't say that. I like being with you."

"Well I like it here. You're not a doctor. You don't know what's wrong with the folks here, or you wouldn't even be talkin' like that." She got up and brushed some grass off her dress. "You won't hear the truth when we tell you. We tried to be civil and even Nurse Watkins has tried, but you keep fighting everything. Travis, you better get used to being here, because getting out isn't as easy as just walking out that gate." The lunchtime bell sounded and Emmie looked up. "Now I'm gonna go me some food. I'm starving. Are you coming with me or not?"

CHAPTER SEVEN

Travis had only gone to his room to get away from everyone else, he didn't intend on falling asleep—especially so early in the afternoon. He was just going to lie on the bed and try to get some logical thinking done. But as his night time sleep was always so vivid and disturbed and far from the relaxed ones he should have, it was no wonder he nodded off.

He woke up with a start. He opened his eyes and didn't feel great. It wasn't anything physical this time. He felt this overwhelming depression sweep over him, his heart ached as though he carried some heavy guilt. This was not the holiday that he'd spent month dreaming of and planning. He got dressed and left his room again, ignoring anyone who passed him or who said hello. He walked down the corridor and stood outside the lift. When it arrived, he went down to the ground floor. He was stifling hot and he needed some air, just a little of that warm breeze to pass his face and bring his determination to understand the things going on. He didn't even look up as he pushed the doors of the entrance open until he realised that he was stepping on grass and not the small gravel stones of the hospital driveway. Then he looked up and almost fainted in shock. He was standing on the grass of the park back home. The park that he'd walked so many times and that was opposite his mother's house. He didn't stop, he didn't hesitate, he ran across the road and knocked on the door. His mother opened it and stood in the doorway—his beautiful, caring, missed mother, with her inviting and warm smile.

"Why did you knock?" she asked. "Where's your key? Don't tell me you've lost it again."

Travis put his hand in his jacket pocket and out came the house key. "I forgot I even had it," he said with a shrug. He lunged forward and threw his arms around his mother, holding her tight. "I've missed you so much."

His mother looked concerned. "What is it Trav? What's troubling you?"

When he heard voices, he walked into the kitchen. His sister and her two children were shouting at each other. When the two boys saw him, they ran over and jumped into his arms. He held them close. He'd never let them go.

"Cuppa?" his sister asked. He looked up at her. She had never looked more beautiful.

"Yeah please, that'd be good." The kitchen looked the same and an intoxicating aroma came from inside the cooker. It was a beef joint cooking, like every Sunday for lunch. He'd missed them. "Where's Dad?" he asked.

"He's in the shed, where else?" his mother said and laughed as she entered the kitchen.

Travis couldn't wait to see him. He walked out into the garden and took a few steps towards the shed. But with each step he took, the shed seemed farther away. He ran toward it, but it moved away from him. He turned to go back into the house and the house was gone. He turned back around to the shed and that was gone too. He closed his eyes and when he opened them again, he was standing outside the hospital. Travis fell to his knees in despair.

Travis gave a loud groan when he opened his eyes. When he was back home, there was a film that he just hated. When it came on, he'd purposely switch the TV over, even though his family loved it and they would roar with laughter each time. The film was about a man who woke up to relive the same day over and over. The man learned to make small changes each day and eventually broke the chain. But Travis couldn't think of anything more annoying than to have the same thing happen to him day after day. It was the same repetitiveness he was having with his job, and it would always be the same problems too. And it was always the same people attached to those problems and with the same arguments and then the same solutions, day in and day out.

Which is the reason why he got out of his chair one Wednesday afternoon and announced he was off to America for a few weeks and when he came back, he wasn't returning to a "sucking the life out of him, nightmarishly boring job."

It was quite ironic when Travis woke up in his room again with the sun shining in his eyes with that familiar music and voice in his head and realised it was again 11:30 a.m. Was he to repeat the same day again too?

He couldn't have been more frustrated. He didn't know which was worse, the dream he'd had about being home when he wasn't, or the nightmare he'd had the night before. That nightmare was the worst yet and it played on his mind more than the others. It felt so real and he couldn't help but think again about what he was still doing there. And why was he being kept there if there was nothing wrong with him? Was it some sort of secret hospital that was doing all sorts of experiments on people they kept drugged? That would explain why he couldn't remember anything and seemed to pass out all the time. He'd read about cults in the US, why shouldn't these types of hospitals be real too? A lone man driving through the US with no one to miss him for weeks. It happened a lot if he could believe the stories.

This time, he was more determined to leave. They had no right to keep him there if he didn't want to stay. He wasn't an American citizen and he legally couldn't be kept against his will.

He wasn't going to do anything different that

would make the staff suspicious of what he was going to do today. He put on his jeans, folded the leg up as high as he could over his knee and put his pyjama bottoms back on so that no one could see his clothes. He did the same for his tee-shirt under his pyjama top and then looked in the mirror to make sure that no part of it was visible. He did up his dressing gown and left the room to make his way down the corridor. He passed the nurses' station where a nurse was more preoccupied in the pill count than in anything else and didn't look up when Travis headed for the stairs. No one seemed interested that he was walking around. He passed the private rooms and didn't stop. He wasn't going to chance a repeat of his dreams by looking in them, he was going to concentrate on getting out. Then he'd bring the authorities back and have the place shut down.

At the bottom of the stairs, one of the cleaners wiped the tiled floors with a drenched mop and didn't bother to acknowledge Travis as he passed him to open the door of the ground floor level. Travis looked both ways, he didn't seem to have raised any suspicion yet. Porters walked around pushing the same patients in wheelchairs and the nurses were busy doing their own thing. No one paid too much attention to him as he continued past the reception area and then straight out of the main entrance to freedom (of a sort) on the other side.

He stood for a few seconds in the sunlight with his face turned up and his eyes closed. It was nice to feel the sun on his face. Ahead of him, still remained the problem of those closed high metal gates and the cameras that visibly pointed to anyone getting close to them on either side. No escape would be possible from there, Travis thought. He walked around the perimeter and examined the wall that surrounded the hospital. Somewhere, there must be a point where no one ventured, or even an area that might have been overlooked in maintenance, or a blind spot to the cameras that were dotted around the hospital.

The wall itself was constructed of brick and covered over with cement and granite stones that had been mixed in with it. They were so sharp that a climb over the wall wasn't an option, you would get cut, scratched or injured and it wasn't going to give you any sort of footing or grip. He looked around the gardens.

Perhaps one of the gardeners had left some tools lying around or something that he could use as a winch to lift himself up and over the wall.

But that was wishful thinking. Of course they wouldn't leave anything just lying around, it was a hospital!

His only way would be to somehow drag one of the benches over and see how high he could build some sort of climbing frame to help him get over it – and without raising any suspicion of what he was doing. Or maybe he could take a look for some rope and a makeshift hook that he could throw over the top and climb over it that way. Perhaps something in the sheds – although they were always kept locked. Maybe he could break into one of them when no one was around... maybe even at night.

He walked around the entire walled area and then did it again. There weren't even any trees nearby that he could climb up on that would give him any sort of leverage in getting him any higher so he could see what was over the wall. No point in scaling the wall only to fall to your death on some barbed wire or sharp points behind it. Although, at this stage, he'd rather be hurt because this facility couldn't cater for such injuries so they'd have no choice but to take him somewhere that could. And then he'd be free.

At first, the sound he heard was like that of heavy winds blowing through the branches and leaves of the trees. Then he saw it, the eerie translucent glow that always seemed to emanate from a group of trancers. They were near luminous as they walked around in formation of three's with at least six rows behind the first lines. Travis hoped that they would just walk past him and ignore he was there, as they continued to stare straight ahead, not focused on anything or anyone. He didn't want them to make "eye" contact with him or anything that would resemble the dream he'd had. But as they got closer, he recognized the faces: the man who stabbed himself, the man who was having sex with the nurse, the man with the hammer and then in the middle of them all—his heart sank—was Emmie.

He pushed his way into the walkers and grabbed her by the arm, but she carried on walking forward. He attempted to pull her out, but there was no budging her. And then they all stopped, like elite, well-trained soldiers. Emmie turned her head and looked at his hand on her arm and then up at him. She smiled, but her eyes were unresponsive, they didn't seem to fully focus on him. She was as pale as the others, her eyes were black and her usually pink lips were grey and chapped. The marks on the side of her forehead were a deeper red, and stood out more against the pale skin. They looked bloody and bruised, as though she'd had more treatment?

"Emmie, we have to leave now!" he shouted. "We can fetch something to put up against the wall and we can climb out of here." He pulled at her arm. "Let's go now while we have the chance. The trancers can shield us from the nurses so they won't be able to see what we'll be doing."

But Emmie just looked at him, confused. Her head moved slightly from side-to-side, but her body didn't move. The trancers turned around and surrounded both of them. And then Emmie finally spoke. Her voice was deep. It wasn't the sweet soft mid-western voice that giggled and wouldn't stop talking. It was a new voice that came from deep within her.

"There's no leaving here," she said. And then the trancers all chanted the same, "There's no leaving here. There's no leaving here."

Two burly porters grabbed Travis from behind and pulled him out from the middle of the group. The trancers regained their formation and the walk began again.

"Where do you think you're doing?" asked one of the porters. "Were you trying to find a way out?" He looked at the other porter. "Yeah, I think he was hoping to find a way out." He looked back to Travis. "Right?"

The other porter whispered in Travis's ear, "You'll never leave here."

CHAPTER EIGHT

Nurse Watkins was sitting behind the desk in her office, when the porters opened her door and pushed Travis into the room.

"He'll be fine." She motioned for them to leave. "I don't need you to stay." As the door closed, she sighed deeply and tutted. "What did you think you were doing? Did you think that we couldn't see you or that we didn't know what you were doing?"

"You sent the trancers to stop me, didn't you?" Travis asked in a raised voice.

"They always take a walk at this time." Her voice was low and calm. "You've just been doing other things."

"Emmie was there."

"Yes, she's moved on, she's joined them now. It's a shame, because we had hopes that she would recover."

"Maybe if you'd stopped giving her electric shock treatments and drugging her, she'd have had a chance."

"It was that treatment and those drugs that kept her going for as long as it did. But her mind wasn't strong enough to keep going. She's slipped farther away and there's nothing anyone can do to help her."

"How about sending her to another hospital? How about sending her somewhere else that specialises in what she has, or what the other trancers have?"

"We do specialise in what they have."

"You keep them here like…like prisoners."

"They're not prisoners. They are here for their own safety."

"Then let me leave. Open that gate and let me leave."

"You don't know where you are yet, do you?"

"I'm in a madhouse—or this is an experimental treatment place—that's where I am. This isn't a hospital and you're not a nurse!"

"You need to sit down."

Travis couldn't control himself any longer. "I don't know how you're doing it. Maybe you drug the food or something so we get hallucinations and nightmares. Maybe you eventually overdose us and we end up as trancers. This is illegal. I'm not American and you can't keep me here if I don't want to stay. And lady, I want out. Now!"

"Travis, sit down," Nurse Watkins said calmly, but with her voice slightly raised.

"What's really going on here?" Travis demanded to know.

Nurse Watkins stared at Travis, then turned - faced the window and looked down at the patients below. Then she turned back to him. "I can see that I'm going to have to tell you everything." She pulled out her chair, sat down and motioned for Travis to do the same. "I don't like to tell our patients any of this because I know it might distress them more than they already are. I get afraid that it might push them farther into their…Well, I feel that if I don't tell you what is happening to you, you're going to try to escape from here again and what's out there is far worse than anything you might find in here. At least here you can wait until…" she stopped herself.

"Until what?" asked Travis. "You need to start telling me everything. I want the truth."

"You're right in a way. This isn't just a hospital. It's a place where people transcend into themselves after a trauma or an accident in your case and that of Emmie."

"Transcend?"

"Between the world we used to live in and sometimes the next. It's a resting place until you are well enough to either go back or until your body tells you it's time to stop… to end."

"So it's a sort of hospice?" asked Travis.

"No… well, yes perhaps, but not entirely. Yes, people do come here that are so far gone there is no hope for them, but they are still clinging onto just the smallest part of their existence. But some, like you for example, will go back soon enough, there are just no guarantees how long that will be."

"I don't understand you. Too far gone? There's no one here at death's door."

"All the trancers are. They are all one step away from death."

"They are walking around, that's hardly death's door."

"Do you remember your accident, Travis?"

"Yes of course. A truck came right at me, but I dodged it. I found your hospital thinking it was a hotel and turned down the road. I should have kept going," he said shaking his head. "I remember all of it. That's why I know I shouldn't be here."

"No, that wasn't everything that happened." she said calmly.

Travis tutted. "Yes it was. Near miss, my car hit the dirt and I..." Travis stopped.

"You can't remember everything after that, can you? But you can remember some. Like a dream, right?"

"I remember driving away after it. I remember the lights that said Hotel... no... it was out, only half of the sign was lit." Travis thought back. It was a mixed up memory but he could remember a face and his car door opening. He could remember being dragged from the car and then heat. He could smell smoke. But he could also remember driving his car down the road. "I don't understand. I have two memories of the same thing and I don't know which is—"

"What do you remember?" she interrupted. "What thoughts do you have? It doesn't matter if they don't make sense to you right now, they all will soon."

Travis sat down. Now he wasn't sure of anything. "I was driving. I wasn't really tired, so I thought I'd carry on." He stopped, trying to remember. "A truck...I remember he crossed over to my side of the road. I swerved and went onto the other side of the road. There was sand. I stopped in the sand. I remember I stopped hard in the sand." He paused for a moment. "That's what I know happened. But I get a few different images every now and again of something else. It doesn't make sense."

"It does, Travis. You're leaving another part of this story out. Do you remember the truck driver?"

"No, he was already gone when I woke up. I mean, I wasn't asleep or unconscious. I just stared out into the night."

"You blacked out?"

"No I didn't. I was in shock because that near miss almost killed me."

"It wasn't a near miss."

"Of course it was. I'd be dead or lying in a hospital bed in plaster, if he'd hit me."

"He clipped you and you spun around a few

times. You hit a rock and the car went over onto its roof. The truck driver opened the door and dragged you out before your car burst into flames. That's what the police told me. There were other witnesses who said the same thing. But it wasn't the truck driver who went over to the other side of the road, it was you. You fell asleep."

Travis remembered a face. He remembered the bright headlamps as they flashed in front of him. He took a deep breath as it all came back to him.

"Your car exploded but he got you out," Nurse Watkins continued. "He called for the highway patrol and when the ambulance arrived, you were already slipping in and out of consciousness. You slipped into your coma before you reached the hospital and a few days later, they brought you here, because this is where people like you stay."

"People like me?" Travis remembered the back of someone's' head again. He remembered lifting his own head and seeing the neon sign. He felt the car turn into the driveway, the gates overhead as he passed through them and the car as it stopped. "I remember the back of a head, so I couldn't have been in an ambulance.

No wait. I remember driving down the road. I remember I was driving the car down the road!" he shouted. "So forget it. You're just planting things into my head that aren't true because you want to keep me here. I'm not falling for it. You and your hospital can go to hell. All you do here is testing on people, like some weird experiment and I'm not going to be part of it. You're not going to experiment on me like you've done to Emmie. You won't make me a trancer however hard you try. I'm leaving and I'm leaving now. You better be prepared to fucking kill me to stop me." Travis got up and forcefully pushed the chair from under him to the ground. He turned and opened the door. "I'm getting out now. This is all bullshit. Me in a coma? I'm walking around, breathing and talking. People in comas are lying on a hospital bed and they don't move, they don't walk around and they don't talk."

"Here in this hospital you're doing all of that. But out there in the real world, you are laying in a bed with your family around you. The voices and the music you hear? That's them. You're down here, deep inside your own consciousness, in a world where you wait until it's time to either go back or go…" She pointed up. "Travis, sit back down and let's talk some more."

But Travis turned and walked out of her office.

Nurse Watkins tutted and shook her head. She picked up the phone and said, "He's heading to the gates, you know what to do."

Travis ran out of the doors and into the daylight again. He could hear footsteps behind him, so he bolted for the gates. The gravel pathways spat up small stones behind him that made him slip down and embed his palms with grit when he landed on them. But the gate was within reach and he wasn't going to hang around. When he reached the gate, he pulled at the rails and hoped that it would just open, but of course it was locked. He tried to get a foot holding on the bars but he slipped down onto the ground on them. Off balance, he fell forward and his arm slipped through the bars. And that's when he saw it—or didn't. His arm completely disappeared when it passed through the bars. He pulled it back in and looked at his hand and then he put it through the bars again. Again, it disappeared. "What the hell? He turned to see the porters who'd caught up with him. In shock, he shouted, "What is this place?"

"Come on Travis," said one of the porters. "You need to come back inside. It'll do you no good being out here."

"Where are we?"

"We're in heaven," said the second porter with a smirk. "And then sometimes we're in hell, and there ain't no leaving either."

Travis screamed through the bars. "Help me! Is anyone out there? Can you hear me?"

The first porter sighed. "Travis, there ain't no leaving here. There's no point in yelling, you'll upset the other patients."

The music began again. Travis screamed, "Turn the fucking music off! I can't stand it any longer."

The porters looked at each other and shrugged. "He's lucky," the first one said to the other, "He can still hear them on the outside. You might end up being one of the lucky ones."

Travis grabbed the first porter by his lapel. "What do you mean, I might be lucky? Lucky in what? Outside?

What's outside? What do you mean?"

"You can hear them on the outside. You still have a link to them. Most here are too far gone or their folks just don't visit them as much anymore. If you can get your folks to hear you, they might be able to bring you back to them."

Travis remembered what Emmie had said one time and he looked at the porter. "Emmie said that we can control lots of things when we're here, we just don't know it," he said.

"Yeah she's kinda right," said the second porter. He came close to Travis's face and sneered. "An' then as we been saying to you, sometimes there just ain't no going back, however hard or loud you wanna scream."

"Come on back to Nurse Watkins's office. She can tell you what you need to hear," said the first porter. "There ain't no point in staying out here." He looked through the gates and then to Travis. "Don't listen to him." He smiled as he pointed at the second porter. "He ain't too kindly because he's stuck here too. But really, there ain't nothing out there. There's just here, until you leave. One way or t'other, you will leave here someday."

Nurse Watkins reached the gates and placed her hand on Travis's shoulder. "I really did try to explain it to you." She looked at the gate. "I remember I did the exact same thing when I first got here." She smiled. "You put your hand through the bars, right?"

Travis nodded.

"And did it disappear?" She raised an eyebrow and shook her head.

He nodded again. "Yes, b-but, I don't get it. I can hear traffic from the freeway. I can hear noises."

"You think we all haven't tried it for ourselves, that we haven't walked around and around this hospital looking for some way out?" She took a step toward the gate, peered through the bars and then turned back to face Travis. "Travis, we're not in the real world anymore. We're in-between life and death and I don't know what to tell you about what's out there, even if we could open the gates to find out. All I know is, I was told to never do it, so I don't."

"Who told you?"

"You know," Nurse Watkins said. "Sometimes you just don't want to ask those questions, you just do as you are told. I ain't gonna upset what we have here. What if we tried to do something about it? What happens to the folks here if it all goes wrong?"

"I don't know. But what if it doesn't go wrong? What if they get a chance to go back home?" Travis asked sharply. "Have you even tried?"

"No, because they'll most likely die quicker and I ain't taking that chance. You want that on your heart? 'Cause I sure don't. These folks, they have a peaceful passing and some do go back. But there ain't no passing those gates. Them's the rules that we stick to."

"Those gates were open when I arrived," he said.

"No they weren't, they are never open. I don't know how it's done. People come here from all parts, it seems. I just know that the phone rings and it tells me to expect a new arrival and then the ambulance is outside by the time I get there. I don't even know who is ringing!"

When Travis looked at Nurse Watkins again, her face had changed. He looked behind him at the porters and theirs had changed too. They were pale, their eyes sunken with deep dark purple bags under each eye. Their lips were an unusual insipid shade of grey, but they weren't trancers, they were something else. Blue veins protruded from their necks and faces, their uniforms were torn and old.

"We're dead. We're probably the only ones here that are dead — me, some of the nurses and all the porters," she said sadly. "We came here a long time back. I was a nurse. It was 1888 and I caught pneumonia. There were many folks sick back then with cancer, because of the dust bowls that used to whip up in their towns and the folks'd get caught up in it. You breathe in that dust for too long and it just burns your lungs away. I was sent from town to town to help in the local hospitals. Tuberculosis was all over some states and had killed all the young 'uns in one town I was sent to. It's a sorrowful journey, when the life of a town is taken like that. It was a bad time and there was no money to treat any of them. Even if we could, their lungs were all but gone to fight it. And then on top of fighting that, one year we got a bout of the flu and pneumonia—nasty it was. If the dust or the tuberculosis didn't get you, the pneumonia did." She took a breath. Her smile was gone, and her eyes teary as she remembered. "I went to sleep for a while and I was lucky, because in my case, I weren't sick for too long. I tried to go back just like you did, I got…had.. a husband and two little uns, but there just ain't no going back when you get as far into the sleep like I was. In the end, though, moments before my passing, I was asked if I wanted to go up"—she motioned to the heavens with her finger—"or did I want to stay and help others with their transition. You see, some folks, well, they die not waking up back in the real world, but while they are here in their transcending stages, I like to make sure they are having a nice time until they get to their end. They eat and drink and keep company with other folks, they get to dance and sing and enjoy the gardens and they can eat whatever their hearts want. It's peaceful and it's enough for many. Some others, well, they're the lucky ones. They wake an' go back to their loved ones. But they don't remember what happened while they were with us — them's the conditions. They just think they slept."

"And me, what about me?" asked Travis.

"Well, we're hoping you're one of the lucky ones. You're different. You have a different aura around you. We saw it when you came in. And you got that plucky attitude that may just get you back someday."

"I don't get it," Travis said. "This place doesn't look old. It's modern. You have cameras at the gates. You have proper medicines and… how can you say you've been here since 1888?"

"The years pass, but they don't mean anything to us. People come and go and leave a little bit of themselves when they visit. We're an old hospital, but some that visit bring their modern touches here too. We've had architects and construction workers and they built this new part. We've had engineers that can make things from old wiring. The cameras, the radios and some things, just appear when we want them. We don't question it. If we think it's going to help here, I pick up the phone and I ask. I mean, within reason, of course." She giggled. "We've had gardeners who work to keep our beautiful gardens growing. Even when some of them have passed on, another takes their place at some point. The section to the far back of us is the original part of the hospital, but it was old and we wanted things to look nice and inviting to make the stay pleasant. Lord knows, being away from your loved ones is traumatic enough."

"Pleasant?"

"If you'd seen the way it looked before. It was old, rundown, cold and damp and it made patients unhappy to be here. And it made them frightened. But now it looks inviting and the patients are happy."

"But they can't leave?"

"Leave to go where? Out there? To the nothingness?" Nurse Watkins took a deep breath. "You still won't accept that it's not possible for everyone to leave here." She stopped for a moment and then nodded, "So I'm going to do something that I have never done for anyone before."

"What's that?"

"I'm going to show you the truth, because telling you the truth, isn't working for you."

CHAPTER NINE

In the El Paso General Hospital, a small, but brightly-lit room, was full of get well cards and flowers and small gifts from friends back home in Wales. They'd started to arrive a few days after Travis was admitted to the hospital after his accident.

Two women were in the room as a nurse entered, followed by a doctor doing his 11:30 rounds. The older woman was short with dark hair and in her middle 50s and in full conversation with a sleeping Travis. "And you'll never guess what Mrs. Harries has been up to. I want you to wake up so I can tell you all our news. I have so much to tell you." She held Travis's hand as the doctor came close. "I know you can hear us, so hurry up."

"Hello, Mrs Williams." He picked up the clipboard that was on a large peg at the end of the bed. "And how is Travis today?"

"I thought I saw his eyelids blinking fast earlier on. I guess he must be having beautiful dreams," she answered.

"Constant eye movement is good. It means his brain is still active."

"Well that's something, eh Cheryl?" She turned to the other woman.

The second woman turned from the window to face them all. Younger and slender, she bore an almost identical resemblance to Travis. "Do you think he'll ever wake up?" she asked sadly.

"I think there's a very good chance he will," the doctor replied, scribbling notes.

"How can you tell?" Cheryl asked.

"Because," the doctor began. "Because I know that there are different degrees of coma. They range from one to five and we have learned that Travis is almost a two, which is good news. Anything between one and three has a good chance of waking up. The problem is, we have no way of telling how long that will take. He still has significant swelling on his brain."

"How about the others that are over three?" Cheryl asked. "What about those?"

"Those that are in the four or five status, to be honest, there's not much chance... I mean, it's rare if they ever come back to us. All we can do for those in that condition is to keep them as comfortable as we can and help them and their families when they do pass."

"I hope you're right about him, then. I miss talking to my brother...and arguing." Her lips curled down at the ends and her eyes began to glaze over until she inhaled deeply and stopped herself from the temptations of balling her eyes out.

The doctor placed his hand on her shoulder. "We will monitor him every day and hope that someday he wakes up and you can come back to take him home." He looked over to Travis and to Mrs. Williams who was talking to Travis again. "When do you have to leave to catch your flights back home?"

"Day after tomorrow, it's going to be so hard to leave him," Cheryl replied. "You know, I was always telling him to shut up and now I want him to shout at me for being annoying."

"When you have things sorted with the insurance companies, we can help you organize his transfer back home. But you never know, you may not even need to do that if he wakes up. And you can call us at any time, it doesn't matter about the time differences. The hospital is staffed twenty-four-seven. You can even Skype us and we'll take the camera straight into his room so we can show you how he's coming along and you can talk to him."

Cheryl couldn't stay in the room any longer. She wanted to cry and let it all out, but her mother stopped her.

"Cheryl, he can probably hear you sniffling, so stop it. I won't have anything sad for him to listen to."

"He can't hear me, Mam. He's in a coma. He can't hear anything!" Cheryl blubbered as she ran out of the room.

"Yes he can," her mother yelled. "The doctors and the nurses all say he can hear everything, so we have to be careful of what we say and of what we do around him."

Cheryl slowly shuffled down the corridor and past the open door of another room where the same doctor had just gone in to check on another patient. He shook his head as he walked out and caught Cheryl as she peeked in to take a look at who the patient was.

"Is she… you know, like my brother?" she asked the doctor.

"Yes," he whispered. "That's Emmie. She's been here just over five years already." He began sadly, "Her condition was re-evaluated to a four this week. Her brain movements have started to show signs of slowing down. They're deteriorating and now she's stopped responding to anything we do. It's unlikely she will ever wake up."

"She looks so young."

"She is and that's the real shame of it too. A truck hit her car. It's like your brother's accident, except that his car landed in sand and hers was sent into a roadside ditch. She was thrown out of her car as it rolled over and then exploded."

"Oh God," Cheryl said, staring down at Emmie. "Poor thing."

"And also, in the case of your brother, we are more hopeful that he will eventually wake up one of these days. But her brain activity decreases each day. She's dying and there's nothing else we can do for her.

We've been giving her mild electronic shockwave treatment to help stimulate her brain activity. It helped her at first. We saw some great improvements in her condition. We were very hopeful when out of the blue one day, she opened her eyes. But soon after, she went back to sleep again and she's not opened them since." He stopped when he saw Cheryl's face. "I'm not saying that this will happen with Travis, of course. But sometimes, I get the feeling that she's just given up on everything, and she's going to stay wherever her unconscious state has taken her. I just hope it's somewhere good." He looked back at Emmie. "She deserves to be somewhere good."

"Do you think Mum is right, that they can hear everything we say?" Cheryl asked him.

"I believe so. There've been several studies over the years to say that those with a higher brain pulse can hear everything."

"Mum is playing the same song over and over again. It's driving me crazy, but she thinks that if he can hear it, then he's enjoying it, because it was one of his favourites. But I hope he'll get so sick of it that it'll make him wake up and go and switch it off himself." She smiled. "Do you think that the music helps them come back?"

"I can't say. But there's no harm in it and it seems to comfort your mother to carry on playing it. She needs that comfort right now, so I'm not going to tell her to stop. I say let her carry on."

Cheryl nodded. "Yeah, I suppose so. It might be driving me up the wall, but listening to it over and over again can't be doing him any harm, can it?"

A scream from down the corridor made both Cheryl and the doctor jump and run out into the corridor. "Cheryl!" screamed Mum. "Quick!"

Cheryl moved like a prize athlete and skidded to a halt as she got to the door, with the doctor close behind. Mum looked up. "He's opened his eyes, Cheryl. He's waking up!"

The doctor took out a small torch from his jacket pocket and waved it in front of Travis's eyes. His pupils didn't dilate or move. "He's not back," the doctor told them. "Sometimes they get a muscle spasm and things happen."

"And then they close them again and never open them, like Emmie, right?" Cheryl asked, concerned.

"Who's Emmie?" asked Mrs. Williams.

"Travis's neighbour in the next room along," Cheryl said.

"This is a good thing, isn't it?" Mrs. Williams asked. "He's opened his eyes, so he knows we're here."

The doctor looked up at them, and then inhaled. "It's a step... a small one, but yes, it's a step further to him coming back. We'll keep him monitored and see if anything further develops. But judging by some of the other patients here, he could close them any time."

"His eyes are open, but can he see us?" Cheryl clarified.

"There's no movement in the eyes, no nerve reaction. I don't think he can," the doctor replied. He sounded disappointed, as if he wanted to deliver positive news.

"Well for now, I'm happy to see those gorgeous brown eyes again," Mum said, holding Travis's hand again.

Travis lay on his bed and closed his eyes. Nurse Watkins was talking shit. What did she mean about showing him? Showing him what? He was trapped there, he really was! He thought about the gates and his arm as it disappeared through the bars. Was her warning justified? Would it ruin everything there if someone got through?

He opened his eyes and heard a loud excited shriek.

And there she was, his beautiful mother, standing over his bed, her face stained with tears as she shouted for the doctors to come. He could see her, he was finally home. But he couldn't move. He lay on the bed and couldn't reach out to her. "Mum! I can see you." Could she hear him? She kept talking over him. She didn't look or listen to him, but yelled for the doctors and for Cheryl to come to the room quickly. Travis shouted again, "Mum, can you hear me?" But still their conversations continued as if they couldn't hear him. "I'm right here, Talk to me!" he shouted as loud as he could.

And then he realised what was going on. This is what Nurse Watkins meant about seeing where he was.

He really was in a coma. He could see the real world, but he couldn't get back into it. His eyes were open, but he wasn't back. He was trapped in the hospital. He was still trapped inside himself.

"Please talk to me!" Travis shouted. "Please help me. I don't want to stay here any longer. Mama, help me. I need to come home."

Travis's eyes closed, leaving the imprint of his mother and her worried face implanted in his head. He could move again. He placed his hands over his face and screamed.

END

ABOUT THE AUTHOR
MARGARITA FELICES

I live in Cardiff, Wales, home to castles, mountains, rugby, Doctor Who and Torchwood, with my partner and three little mad dogs and I work for a well-known TV broadcasting company. I love living in Cardiff because, for all its modernisation, there are still remnants of an old Victorian city. I love writing and will always base my stories in Cardiff because it has such character. When I can, I go out to the coast and take photographs, we have a lovely castle in the city centre and a fairytale one just on the outskirts, so when I feel I can't write anything, I take a ramble to those locations and it clears my head.

I have a TV production background. I used to be a professional photographer and decided to move into the TV world. I started off working on our local news programmers' and then moved on to Arts, Factual, Drama, back to Factual, back to Drama (Torchwood, Dr Who and a few regional shows). And I'm currently working on scripting the JOS series in the hopes of getting them into production very soon. I now work for the BBC National Orchestra or Wales and we produce some of the music for well-known TV shows, Doctor Who for example! I've learnt so much about Marketing and Promotions. It's been an absolute blessing.

But I suppose it was inevitable that someday I would write novels. My teachers at school used to limit me to no more than ten pages. I was a reporter on the school magazine and later became its Editor. When I left school, I paid my way through college by writing short stories for magazines; I later took a course in scriptwriting and came third in a BBC writing competition. I am Gothic; I love the fashion, the architecture and the music. The club in my novel, Judgement of Souls 3, is real. The rock star in my novel Ordinary Wins is real… I like to incorporate people that I know in my novels, it's so much fun!

YOU CAN CONNECT WITH MARGARITA HERE:

https://www.facebook.com/JudgementOfSouls3TheKissAtDawn/

https://www.facebook.com/felicm60/

https://www.instagram.com/felicm60/

https://www.youtube.com/watch?v=g5H_GL2Z0xI&feature=em-share_video_user

https://www.youtube.com/watch?v=hbCvxTqdlAQ&t=52s

https://www.youtube.com/watch?v=Gc1avY_XDvk

https://twitter.com/felicm60

Books to Go Now

You can find more stories such as this at www.bookstogonow.com

If you enjoyed this Books to Go Now story, please leave a review for the author on the review site where you purchased the eBook. Thanks!

We pride ourselves with representing great stories at low prices. We want to take you into the digital age, offering a market that will allow you to grow along with us in our journey through the new frontier of digital publishing.

Some of our favorite award-winning authors

have joined us. We welcome readers and writers into our community.

We want to make sure that as a reader, you are supplied with never-ending great stories. As a company, Books to Go Now, wants its readers and writers supplied with positive experiences and encouragement, so they will return again and again.

We want to hear from you. Our readers and writers are the cornerstone of our company. If there is something you would like to say or a genre that you would like to see, please email us at inquiry@bookstogonow.com

Printed in Great Britain
by Amazon